W9-CCA-978

Little Cliff's First Day of School

◆ CLIFTON L. TAULBERT ◆ paintings by E. B. LEWIS ◆

PUFFIN BOOKS

PUFFIN BOOKS
Published by Penguin Group
Penguin Young Readers Group,
345 Hudson Street, New York, New York 10014, U.S.A.
Penguin Books Ltd, 80 Strand, London WC2R ORL, England
Penguin Books Australia Ltd, 250 Camberwell Road, Camberwell, Victoria 3124, Australia
Penguin Books Canada Ltd, 10 Alcorn Avenue, Toronto, Ontario, Canada M4V 3B2
Penguin Books (N.Z.) Ltd, 182-190 Wairau Road, Auckland 10, New Zealand

First published in the United States of America by Dial Books for Young Readers,
a division of Penguin Putnam Inc., 2001
Published by Puffin Books, a division of Penguin Young Readers Group, 2003

1 3 5 7 9 10 8 6 4 2

THE LIBRARY OF CONGRESS HAS CATALOGED THE DIAL EDITION AS FOLLOWS:
Taulbert, Clifton L.
Little Cliff's first day of school / by Clifton L. Taulbert;
pictures by E. B. Lewis.
p. cm.
Summary: Little Cliff is terrified of starting school, but with Mama Pearl's
encouragement, he is able to overcome his fears.
ISBN: 0-8037-2557-4 (hc)
[1. First day of school—Fiction. 2. Schools—Fiction. 3. Fear—Fiction. 4. Great-grandmothers—Fiction.]
I. Lewis, Earl B., ill. II. Title.
PZ7.T2114215 Lk 2001 [E]—dc21 99-056115

Puffin Books ISBN 0-14-250082-8

Printed in the United States of America
The full-color artwork was prepared using watercolors.

Dedicated to Anne Kathryn Taulbert,
"Forever My Inspiration"
C.L.T.

To Jeff and Elizabeth,
Thank you for the foresight
E.B.L.

Tomorrow was the first day of school in Little Cliff's town. His great-grandmother, Mama Pearl, was very happy. His great-grandfather, Poppa Joe, was also happy. Their faces were all smiles as they laid out Cliff's new clothes on their big iron bed: blue jeans, a plaid woolen shirt, brown shoes, a pair of knee-high stockings, and a green corduroy cap with long flaps. The calendar said September, so Mama Pearl ignored the hot Delta sun and dressed Little Cliff for the fall.

The whole house was happy, except for Little Cliff. He didn't want to go to Miss Maxey's school. He didn't want to wear the knee-high stockings or the new cap with the long flaps. He wanted to stay home with his great-grandparents, just as he'd done all his life.

When Mama Pearl said it was time to try on his new brown shoes, Cliff pretended that he couldn't get them on. He sat in the big chair and pulled hard on the shoes, but they kept falling to the floor. Then he sat on the floor and lifted his feet high in the air and pretended to huff and puff. "Mama, these shoes too little. I can't go to school now," he said.

"Too little? Why, boy, I can get two of y'all in them shoes," Mama Pearl said. She stood over Little Cliff and pointed her finger at the shoes on the floor. "Cliff, don't step on my nerves. Now you git them shoes on right now."

Cliff knew that when Mama Pearl stopped laughing, it was time to stop pretending. He slowly picked up the shoes, and just like that, they went on.

"You see, baby? Mama knew it. Them shoes was made for yore two feet." Mama Pearl was happy again, but Cliff was still sad. He did not want to start first grade—not one bit.

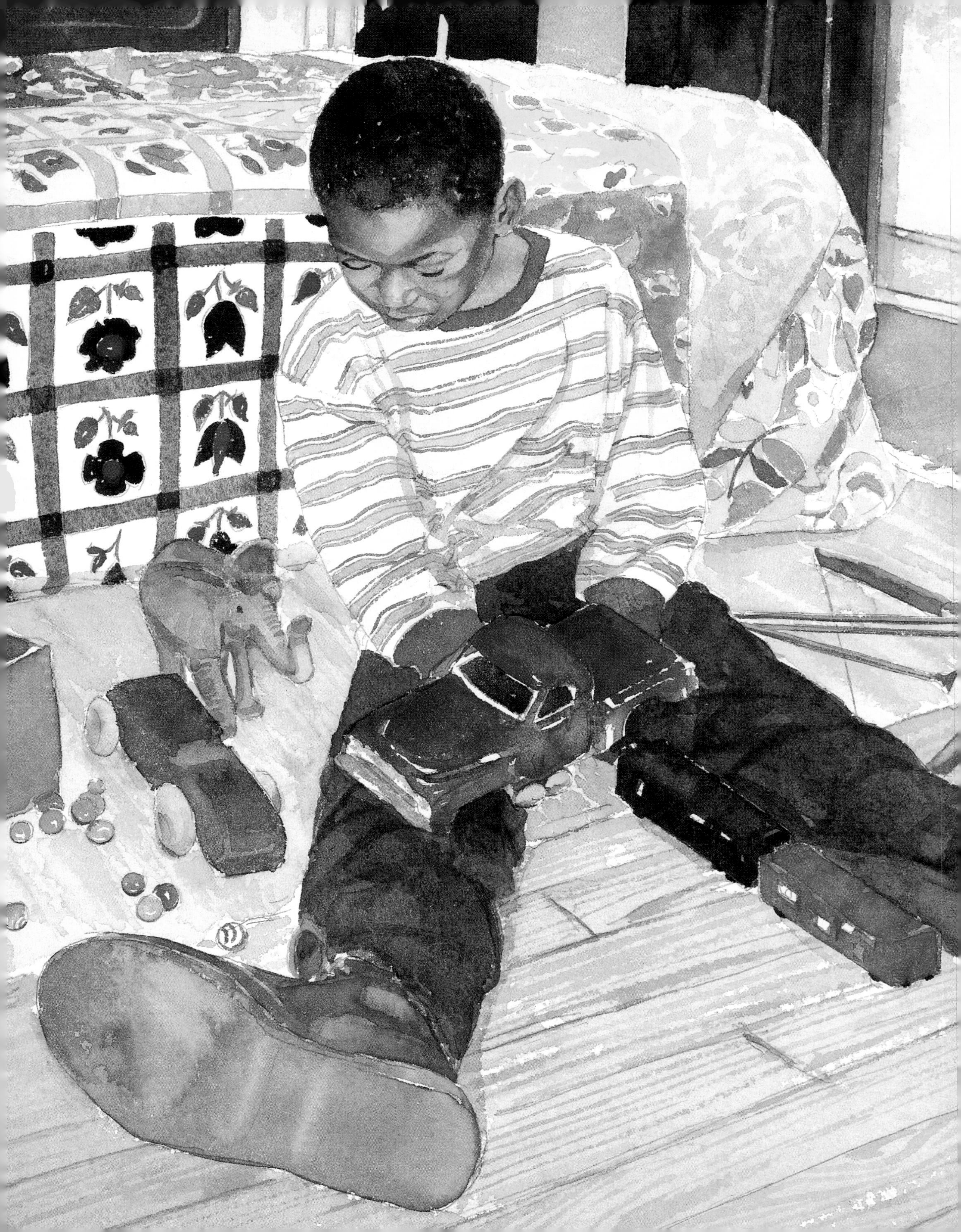

All afternoon, Little Cliff gathered his toys and placed them on the floor around his bed. As he put them side by side, he talked to each one: iron trains, trucks without wheels, a bow-and-arrow set, and his shoe box full of marbles. "I can't play with y'all no more. I gotta go to Miss Maxey's school way down the road, a million miles from here. I know you gonna miss me, 'cause I miss y'all already."

By bedtime, he was worn out, but he could hardly sleep. He kept thinking about tomorrow. Mama Pearl said he would have to sit quietly and listen to the teacher. Mr. Boot-Nanny, his neighbor, had given him a new cornbread writing tablet with coarse brown sheets of paper and heavy black lines. His Sunday-school teacher, Mother Byrd, had given him two new lead pencils, but not before saying, "We expect you to work, work, work."

Only big people like school, he thought. Finally he covered his head with his quilt and went to sleep.

The next morning, Little Cliff was awakened by the smell of hot grits and cured ham. His new clothes were waiting for him on his chair. He dressed slowly, finally pulling on his knee-high stockings and brown shoes. Then he quietly walked out to the sunporch.

"Aw, baby, you look so good to Mama," his great-grandmother said as she looked him over from head to toe. Poppa Joe patted him on the head as he placed his breakfast plate in front of him.

Cliff sat down, but he only picked at his food. "Poppa, I'm scared," he said.

"Oh, now, there's nothing for Poppa's little man to be scared of," his Poppa said. He looked at Mama Pearl, and they both shook their heads as if they didn't know what to do.

Little Cliff asked to be excused from the table. He ran to the backyard where he kept his number-three tub parked under the side of the house. Kneeling on the ground, he pulled out the old tub.

"Number three, my good ol' car, gonna miss you. Can't drive to see the world anymore. Can't go 'round and 'round this big ol' house. I hafta go to school and work, work, work." He rubbed the tub on its shiny sides and then walked over to his favorite chinaberry tree.

The old tree was as tall as the house, and Little Cliff had played in it as long as he could remember. He loved it most of all in the summertime, when the leaves were bright and shiny and so thick, he could hide from the sun. He would sit on the strong lower branch, gather handfuls of the hard green chinaberries, and throw them at all the chickens that crossed his path.

Today Cliff looked up at the big branch that seemed to be bending down to hear him speak. "I'll miss you, ol' tree, so tall and strong. I hafta go to school and be quiet, quiet, quiet."

"Baby, baby, Cliffy, where's you, boy?" Mama Pearl called from the sunporch. "Time's a-movin'! You gotta grab yore new school stuff. Yessir, Mama's baby is gonna be a little 'fessor."

Cliff climbed the back stairs and went into the sunporch, where both Poppa Joe and Mama Pearl were waiting for him. Poppa Joe gave him his new tablet and the two pencils, and Mama Pearl gave him his lunch bucket. Then Little Cliff began to cry big tears that ran down his chubby face like raindrops. He didn't want to leave his great-grandparents and everything he loved. He didn't want to be a 'fessor. He just wanted to stay home.

"That's all right, son, you gonna be just fine. I can feel it in my bones," said Poppa Joe, giving him a big bear hug. "Time to scat, boy."

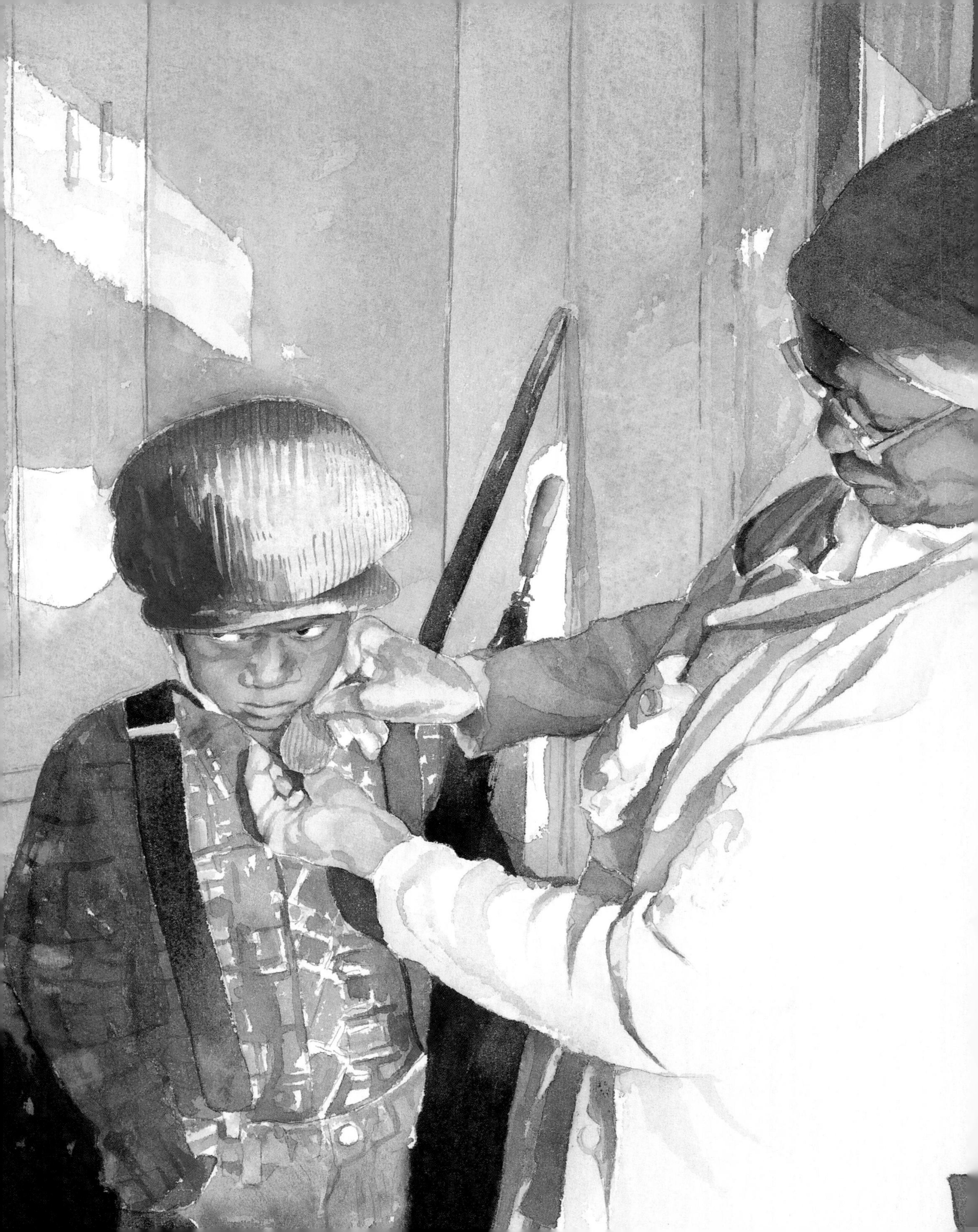

Little Cliff dragged his feet as he walked through the house. He dropped a pencil on the floor and tried to hide his green corduroy cap. But Mama Pearl was right behind him, picking up his pencil and grabbing the cap from under the chair. As Cliff opened the screen door, Mama Pearl stopped him and pulled the cap over his head, tying the flaps tightly under his chin.

Little Cliff stood on the big front porch. He was all dressed and ready for school, but he didn't move.

"I better walk you to Miss Maxey's school myself," Mama Pearl said firmly. She took his hand and led him down the tall steps and into the front yard.

Cliff broke free and scooted right under the house. When the sun was real hot, he liked to play there, near the base of the chimney, where the air was cool and the dirt was soft. But today he was not playing. He was hiding.

Mama got on her knees and called, "Cliffy, boy, you'd better git here this very minute. I told Miss Maxey you'd be at school, and true to my word, boy, you gonna be thar if I have to load you on my back. Come on outta thar right now."

When Cliff heard "right now," he knew Mama Pearl meant business, so he crawled out from under the house. He was all covered with spiderwebs and dirt. Mama Pearl dusted him clean with her palm. Then she grabbed his hand and headed down the blacktop road to Miss Maxey's school.

Cliff clung tightly to his great-grandmother. Though a big boy, he walked close to her, even trying to hide his face in her big apron. As they drew near the school, he heard the sounds of laughter and dogs barking. He pulled his head from behind Mama Pearl's apron. There were all his friends, dressed for the first day of school: his cousin Bobby; his friend Frank, Mr. Will's grandson; Miss Laura's boy, Bubba; and Laughin' Earl from up the road.

Everyone seemed to shout at once: "Hey, Cliffy, you gonna sit by me." "Cliff, what you got in your lunch bucket? You wanna swap?" "I brought my bat, we gonna play baseball at recess." "Did you bring your new ball?"

Cliff could hardly believe his eyes and ears. All he'd heard about school was work, work, work and quiet, quiet, quiet. Nobody had told him you could have *fun* at school!

He quickly dropped Mama Pearl's hand, jerked off his green cap, and ran ahead to meet his friends. Mama Pearl laughed. "Cliffy!" she yelled. "The schoolhouse is in front of you, not over there."

When he looked back, she held up his lunch bucket, the tablet, the pencils, and the cap. "Give 'em to the teacher," he yelled. "This is a fun place after all!"

Miss Maxey was standing beyond the big open doorway of the white wooden building. She spoke to Mama Pearl and smiled as she placed Little Cliff's lunch and supplies in the pile that was growing around her feet.

As Mama Pearl walked away, Cliff ran to hug her and was surprised to see her wiping the corner of her eye on her apron. "Mama, why you crying?" he asked. "You wanna go to school?"

Now Mama Pearl was laughing and crying. She reached down and gave Little Cliff a big, big hug. "No, no, baby, Mama can't stay. I am just so happy we made it to school on our first day," she said.

Little Cliff waved and ran back to play. Mama Pearl stood at the edge of the schoolyard, holding the green corduroy cap in her hands. She stood for a while and watched the children playing, her face beaming with pride. Then, slowly, she made her way home.

And Little Cliff, now laughing with his friends, went inside the schoolhouse to learn.